MY FRIEND and I

Lisa Jahn-Clough

HOUGHTON MIFFLIN COMPANY BOSTON

Walter Lorraine  Books

For my friend Matt

Walter Lorraine (wr) Books

Copyright © 1999 by Lisa Jahn-Clough

Library of Congress Cataloging-in-Publication Data

Jahn-Clough, Lisa.
    My friend and I / Lisa Jahn-Clough.
        p.   cm.
    Summary: A young girl makes friends with the new boy next door,
and when they have a fight, she discovers that she misses him.
    ISBN 0-395-93545-8
    (1. Friendship—Fiction.)   I. Title.
PZ7.J153536My   1999
[E]—DC21   98-30519
                                                               CIP
                                                                AC
Printed in Singapore
TWP 10 9 8 7 6 5 4 3

Once upon a time there was me.

I played with my toys.

Until one day a little boy
moved in next door.

U LUG IT

The little boy asked,
"What are you doing?"
"Watching," I said.
"Do you have any toys?" he asked.
"Yes," I said.
"Me, too. Let's play!"

We lined up all of our toys.

We had three dolls, two cars,
four trucks, two bears, one lion,
six balls, two soldiers, and some string.

One day my friend had a new toy.
"It's soft and new and mine," he said.
"I want to play with it," I said.
He held the bunny tight. "No," he said.

We had three dolls, two cars,
four trucks, two bears, one lion,
six balls, two soldiers, and some string.

We wore silly hats and blew up balloons.

We played the drums and danced.

We sang songs and jumped in the air,
"You're my friend," he said.
"You're my friend too." I said.
We were very happy.

One day my friend had a new toy.
"It's soft and new and mine," he said.
"I want to play with it," I said.
He held the bunny tight. "No," he said.

I tried to grab the bunny.
My friend grabbed it back.
I shouted, "I want it!"
My friend yelled back, "No!"
I pulled the bunny.
My friend pulled it back.
We grabbed and shouted
and yelled and pulled.

Until suddenly . . .

the bunny broke!

"Uh-oh," I said.
"You're not my friend anymore,"
my friend said. "Go away."

I played by myself again.

I lined up my toys. I wore my
silly hat. I danced. I sang.

But it wasn't the same.

I peeked in the window.
He was trying to fix the bunny.
"What are you doing?" he asked.
"Watching," I said.
"Oh," he said.
"I think I can help," I said.
"How?" he asked.

I showed him what we could do.
Together we fixed the bunny
almost as good as new.
"I'm sorry I broke your bunny," I said.
"It doesn't look so bad now," he said.

"I missed you," I said.
"I missed you too," he said.
"Friends again?" I asked.
"Friends," my friend said.
"Now let's fix all our toys!"

And so we did,

my friend and I.